Tales from Old Ireland

retold by
Malachy Doyle

illustrated by
Niamh Sharkey

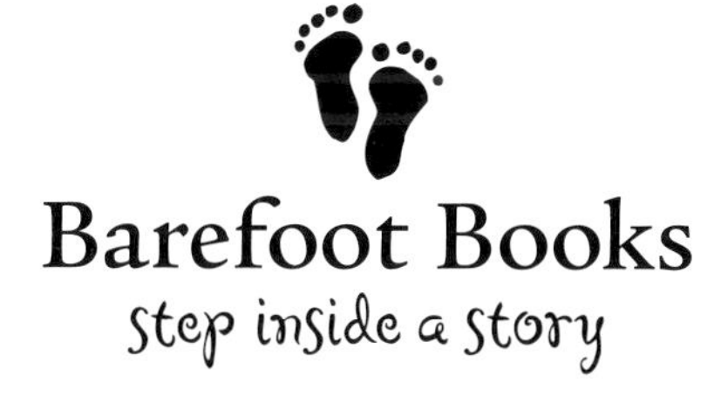

In memory of my mother, Eileen Mary Doyle — M. D.

For Emer and Caoimhe — N. S.

Barefoot Books
2067 Massachusetts Ave
Cambridge, MA 02140

Barefoot Books
29/30 Fitzroy Square
London, W1T 6LQ

First published in Great Britain by Barefoot Books, Ltd
and in the United States of America by Barefoot Books, Inc in 2000
This paperback edition first published in 2017

Graphic design by designsection, England
Reproduction by Grafiscan, Italy
Printed in China on 100% acid-free paper
This book was typeset in ITC Berkeley Oldstyle
The illustrations were prepared in oil and gesso on canvas

ISBN: 978-1-78285-358-9

British Cataloguing-in-Publication Data:
a catalogue record for this book is available from the British Library

Library of Congress Cataloging-in-Publication Data
is available under LCCN 2005022543

1 3 5 7 9 8 6 4 2

There is an old Irish proverb, "A tune is more precious than birdsong, and a tale more precious than the wealth of the world." As a child growing up in Whitehead, a quiet little town near Belfast, I was well aware that folk tales were some of my most precious possessions. I heard them, and later read them, as often as I could, and I love them still.

The Irish oral tradition is one of the richest in the world — stories have been told around our firesides for thousands of years and the tradition has never died. Some of the myths and legends, folk and fairy tales told now are the same ones that were heard in the times of the early Celts, long before Christianity came to Ireland. Others were written down by monks as early as the seventh century, but most were passed on solely by word of mouth. In the nineteenth century, people began to collect and publish the songs and stories that had survived, gathering them from the country people, mainly in the Irish language.

When the Irish Folklore Commission was set up in the 1930s, one of the ways it went about its job was to encourage schoolchildren to ask the oldest people in their area to tell them their stories. The greatest collection of folklore in the world was thus assembled, and it is now held at University College, Dublin.

Irish folk tales have a magic and a simplicity, a depth and a passion that appeal to people of all ages and nationalities. They have survived so long because of the great enjoyment they give both in the hearing and the telling. They are full of action and rhythm, with little description to slow them down. In Ireland, a story is rarely told the same way twice, so that you can hear or tell it many times and never feel bored. While some of the early heroic tales can be fairly gruesome, others are full of emotion and feeling, and there is a great strand of comedy running through many of them.

This collection contains many of my most treasured stories. I have retold them freely, as was always the way. Try reading them aloud — that's how they work best.

Malachy Doyle

Contents

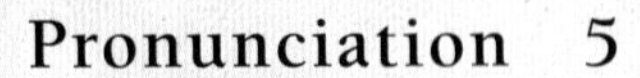

Pronunciation

(Underlining indicates emphasis)

Aed	ee
Aherlow	ah-her-<u>low</u>
Aidan	<u>ey</u>-dan
Aoife	<u>ee</u>-fuh
Bevin	bey-veen
Cahir	care
Cappagh	<u>kapp</u>-a
Connacht	<u>konn</u>-ukt
Cormac	<u>kor</u>-mac
Craic	crack
Erin	<u>air</u>-in
Fiacra	<u>fee</u>-ak-ra
Fionn Mac Cumhail	finn ma-cool
Fionnuala	fin-<u>noo</u>-la
Inish Glora	inn-ish <u>glor</u>-a
Leinster	<u>len</u>-ster
Lir	lur
Lorcan	<u>lor</u>-kan
Niamh	<u>nee</u>-uv
Oisín	ush-een
poteen	puh-<u>cheen</u>
Tara	<u>tar</u>-a
Tír Chonaill	<u>teer</u> kon-ill
Tuatha Dé Danaan	<u>tooa</u>-ha juh <u>dan</u>-an
Tír na nÓg	<u>teer</u> na <u>noag</u>

The Children of Lir

In Ireland long ago there was a king called Lir. He was one of the Tuatha Dé Danaan, a mighty and magical race, and he had a charming wife and four lovely children. Fionnuala was the eldest, the only girl, and she was as beautiful as sunshine in blossomed branches. Aed was like a young eagle in the sky, and Fiacra and Conn, the two youngest, were as cheerful as bubbling streams.

Everything was as it should be, until the queen took sick and died. The king's heart was broken, and the children missed their mother every minute of the day. They missed her games, her songs and stories, and most of all they missed her love.

Lir could see that they were sad, but he did not know how to help them. He decided to find a new wife as soon as possible, for he could not bear to be alone and his children needed a mother.

And so it was that when he met Aoife, a stranger to those parts, he was struck by her beauty and blind to her evil. For Aoife was a witch, and as soon as she saw how much love the king had for his four children, she hated them. With every bone of her body and every hair of her head, she hated them.

"Come for a ride in my chariot, dear children," she said one day. And when they arrived at the loneliest place in the province, she ordered the horseman to kill them.

"I shall not!" cried the man, but Aoife knocked him to the ground and drove on. When they arrived at the Great Lake, she ordered the children into the water. No sooner had they entered than she struck each one with her rod of enchantment, turning them into four swans.

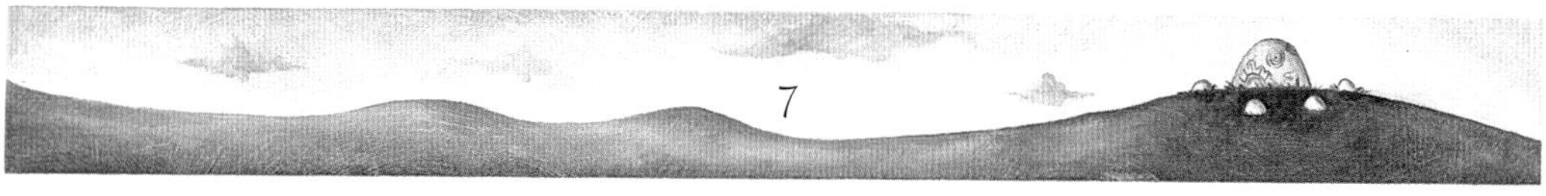

"For three hundred years you will swim on this lake," she gloated, "and then you will fly to the cold Sea of Moyle. For another three hundred years you will shiver and suffer, before you can go to the Sea of Erris, for the final three hundred years!"

"You are a wicked woman and my father will punish you!" Fionnuala cried.

But Aoife only laughed. "You must wait until a druid with a shaven crown comes over the seas and you hear the sound of a bell, ringing for prayers. Only then will your exile be over," she said.

"Will you do nothing to lighten our sorrow?" pleaded Fionnuala. "Surely not even you are so cruel?"

"You shall keep the power of speech and thought," answered the cruel queen, "and you will be able to sing more beautifully than the world has ever heard. That is all I shall give you."

When the horseman returned to Lir to tell him what had happened, the king flew into a terrible rage. He called for his horse, summoned his men and rode out to find them. As he passed by the Great Lake, Fionnuala and her brothers cried out to him and deep was his grief when he saw them.

"Come to me, my children," he said, stroking their feathers. "I cannot give you back your shapes till the curse is ended, but come home with me and I shall try to make your lives more bearable."

"We are unable to leave this lake, Father," said Fionnuala. "And anyway, how could we return to the castle? Our stepmother

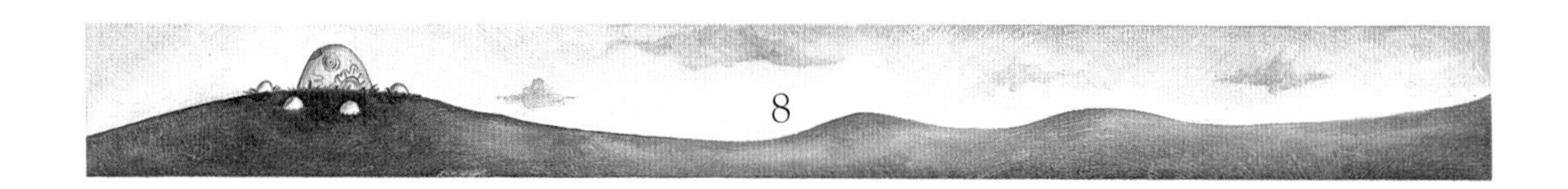

will be there and it would pain us to the heart to see her again."

At that moment, Lir spotted Aoife hiding behind a rock, laughing slyly.

"Begone, you creature of the night!" he yelled, conjuring up his own magic. "Fierce winds will drive you to the restless places of the earth, and you will lose all your beauty. Your punishment will be worse than the one you have put upon my children, for at least theirs will cease after nine hundred years. Yours will continue until the end of time!"

Then he turned Aoife into a demon, and with a howl of terror she vanished. That night, Lir and his men stayed by the lake, listening to the swans. Their songs were more beautiful than any the world had ever heard.

The king made a law that no one in Ireland should kill a swan, for fear it might be one of his children. He promised a reward to anyone who could break the spell, but although many tried, no one succeeded. So every evening, King Lir would ride out to the Great Lake to speak to his children, and to hear their beautiful songs.

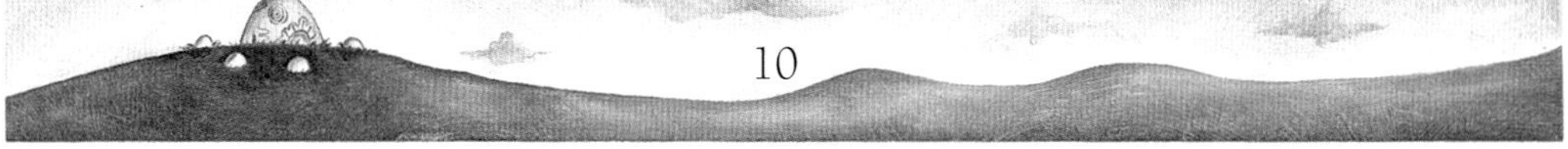

The king's heart was sorely broken. First he had lost his beloved queen, and now he had lost his sons and his daughter. Slowly the years passed, and one night he came to the lake to say goodbye, for he knew that he would not last another day.

"Farewell, my lovely children," he said. "My blessings be upon you, till the sea loses its salt and the trees forget to bud in springtime. Farewell, Fionnuala, my blossom; Aed, my eagle of the sky; and Conn and Fiacra, who brought me gladness always. May you find joy at the end of your troubles."

And with that he lay down and died, and the four swans took to the air and circled around him, keening.

As time went on, more and more people heard about the swans. They flocked to the Great Lake, and all who heard their music were cured of their illness, pain, or sorrow.

When the first three hundred years had passed, long after all the people who had known Lir and his children were gone, Fionnuala told her brothers that the time had come to fly north.

Into the air they rose, and far away they flew, and they never rested once till they came to the narrow Sea of Moyle that flows between Ireland and Scotland. A cold, stormy sea it was, and lonely, and there was no one to listen to their singing. They had little heart for song anyway, as the bitter waves tossed them this

way and that, dashing them against sharp rocks when they tried to shelter near the shore. The winds from the north lashed their feathers with ice, and in winter snow whirled so densely they could hardly see.

In the pale mornings, Fionnuala would gather her brothers under her wings and comfort them, but the three hundred sad and hungry years seemed forever, and even she was in danger of forgetting the songs of their childhood and the days when life was good.

When, at last, they could leave the Sea of Moyle, Fionnuala said to her brothers, "It is time for us to fly once more. We must seek the western sea, the Sea of Erris."

First they flew south and then they flew west, until they came to the island of Inish Glora. The wild Atlantic was cold, but summer brought gentle winds and sunshine to warm their aching bones. Fionnuala kept her brothers' spirits up by singing the songs

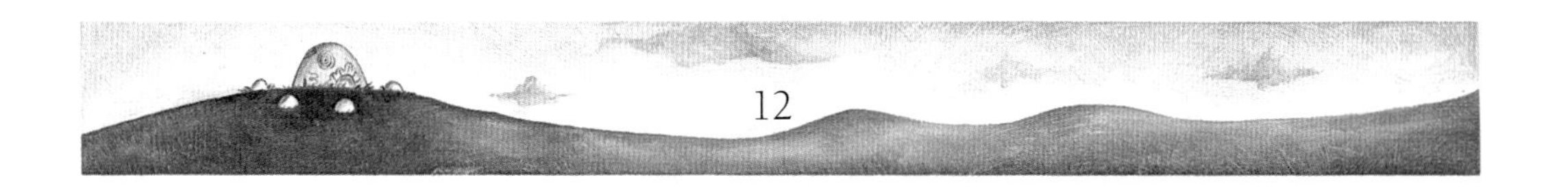

of their youth, and by reminding Aed, Fiacra and Conn that the spell was slowly coming to an end, and in time they would be free.

When the last three hundred years had passed, Fionnuala said to her brothers, “Let us fly to our father’s house, to see how his people are.”

They were all day flying, for age and storm had slowed their wings, and at last they came to their old home. When they looked down they saw no light, they heard no music. The gorgeous house, the white hounds, and the beautiful horses had disappeared. All they found was a mound of grass and nettles.

“Beauty is gone from the earth, brothers,” said Fionnuala, lamenting. “We have no home.”

All night the Children of Lir lay in the long grass, silent with grief. When they felt the warmth of morning, they rose in the air and flew in wide circles, seeking their people. On the plains where the Tuatha Dé Danaan had hunted silver-horned stags, all they could see were the dwellings of strangers, tending flocks and sowing corn.

"Let us return to the isle of Inish Glora, my brothers," said Fionnuala. "For at least we shall have the warm winds of summer on our backs. And in time a bell, ringing for prayers, will lighten our sorrow."

So they returned to the Sea of Erris, and in the shelter of the island they sang quietly to each other and waited.

And one evening, as the sun set, Fionnuala lifted her head, listening. Yes, there it was again, the clear, sweet ringing of a bell.

"Surely this is the sound we've been waiting for!" she cried.

They followed the noise up a grassy path, until they came to a small church. An old monk came out, and was startled to meet four swans on the doorstep.

"What are you doing here, birds?" he asked, scratching his head.

"We've come to hear your bell," replied Fionnuala.

The monk jumped back, amazed to hear her speak, but Fionnuala told him their story, and all that their stepmother, Aoife, had done.

"What a terrible life you've had, poor creatures," said the monk. "It was the sound of Patrick's bell you heard. He has gone away

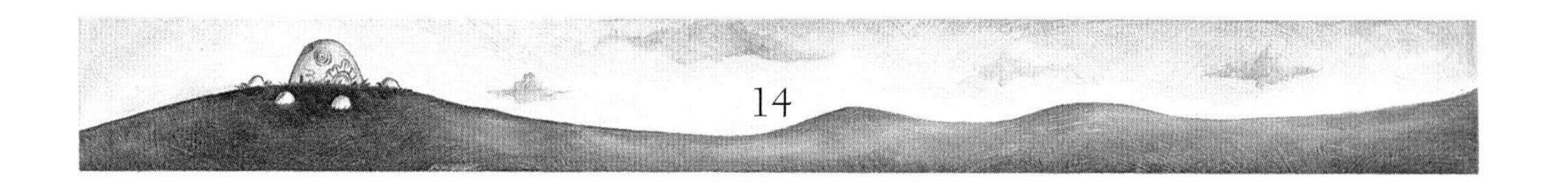

from here, leaving me to tend his church, but I know that he would want me to take care of you."

The holy man went inside the church and brought out some holy water, which he sprinkled on the swans while he prayed.

As soon as the water touched them, their feathers fell away and Fionnuala and her brothers were human again. But they were over nine hundred years old, and so they died. The monk dug a grave and buried them side by side, close to his little church.

At last they were together again, King Lir, his good wife and their four children.

Fair, Brown and Trembling

A long time ago, before you were born, or your grandmother was born, or your great-great-grandmother before her, there was a king in Tír Chonaill and he had three daughters, Fair, Brown and Trembling.

Fair and Brown had new dresses whenever they wished, and went to church every Sunday. But Trembling, the youngest, was kept at home to clean and cook. Her sisters wouldn't let her out of the house at all, for she was by far the most beautiful of the three, and they were afraid she might marry first.

This went on for seven long years, and at the end of the seventh year the son of the King of Omanya began to show an interest in the eldest sister.

One Sunday morning, after Fair and Brown had gone to Mass, the old henwife came into the kitchen. "You ought to be in church, girl," she said to Trembling, "instead of working here at home."

"How can I go?" answered Trembling. "My clothes are in rags, and if my sisters saw me, they'd kill me for leaving the house."

"I'll give you a finer dress than either of those two lumps has ever seen," said the henwife, "for they're not fit to kiss the ground you walk on. Now what would you like?"

"Don't tease me, Henny," said Trembling, with a smile. "But if you want to know what I wear in my dreams, it's a dress as white as the winter snow, with emerald shoes for my feet."

The henwife put on a magic cloak of darkness and took out her scissors. She clipped a piece from Trembling's rags, and called for the whitest robes in the world and a pair of emerald-green shoes.

When the girl was dressed and ready, the henwife said, "I have a honey-bird here to sit on your right shoulder, and another for your left. At the door stands a milk-white mare, with a golden bridle to hold in your hand and a golden saddle to ride on."

Trembling sat on the golden saddle, and when she was ready to ride, the henwife said, "Whatever you do, dear, don't go inside the door of the church. And the minute they rise at the end of Mass, fly away as fast as the mare will carry you."

When Trembling came to the church, the people were amazed at the sight of the beautiful stranger. They were pushing and shoving to get a better view, and when Trembling galloped away at the end they ran after her. But there was no good in the chasing, for she outstripped the wind before and the wind behind, and she was away before man or beast could draw near.

Arriving home, Trembling found the henwife had dinner ready. She took off the white robes, put on her rags, and when the two sisters came back, the old woman asked them, "Have you any news from the church this morning?"

"We've terrible news!" said they. "There was a grand lady came to the door. You've never seen the like of her robes, and nobody

so much as glanced at us. There wasn't a man, from king to beggar, who wasn't trying to see who she was."

From that day on, the sisters gave no one a minute's peace till they had two dresses like the robes of the strange lady, though honey-birds were nowhere to be found.

The next Sunday, Fair and Brown went to church again, leaving Trembling at home. After they had gone, the henwife came in.

"Are you off to church today, young Trembling?"

"I'd love to, Henny," said the girl, "if I'd something to wear."

"What would you have?" asked the old woman.

"Oh, the finest black satin that can be found, shimmering with pearls," said Trembling, dreamily, "and ruby shoes for my feet."

"What kind of mare would you have, dear?"

"One so black and so glossy that I could see myself reflected in her body," answered the girl.

The henwife put on the cloak of darkness, called for the robes and the mare, and that moment she had them. The saddle was silver and so was the bridle, and when Trembling was dressed,

the henwife put a honey-bird on each shoulder.

"Remember," said the old woman, "don't go inside the door of the church, and be sure to leave before any man can stop you."

That Sunday, the people were more astonished than ever. They gazed at the beautiful stranger the whole way through Mass, and all they were thinking was to know where she had come from. But the moment they rose at the end, she hurried away on the mare.

Trembling took off the satin robe and was back in her rags before the sisters got home.

"What news have you today, girls?" asked the henwife.

"Awful news!" said they. "The grand lady was back, and not a soul noticed us in our beautiful dresses, what with the satin robes she had on. All the church, from high to low, had their mouths open, gaping at her. Even the priest!"

The two sisters didn't rest till they had dresses as close to the stranger's robes as they could find. But they weren't a patch on them, to tell you the truth, for the likes of those could never be found in Ireland.

So when the third Sunday came, Fair and Brown went to church dressed all in black. They left Trembling at home to work in the kitchen, and told her to be sure and have dinner ready when they got back.

As soon as they were out of sight, the henwife came in.

"Well, dear, are you off to Mass?" said she.

"I would if I'd a new dress, Henny," smiled Trembling.

"I'll get you any dress you want," said the henwife. "What would you like?"

"Oh, I've been thinking about that," said Trembling, laughing. "I'd like a gown as red as a rose from the waist down, and white as snow from the waist up. I'll have a cape of green on my shoulders; a hat of red, white and green feathers on my head; and shoes for my feet with the toes red, the middle white, and the back green."

"You'll be a sight for sore eyes!" said the henwife, throwing on the cloak of darkness and producing the clothes. When Trembling was dressed, the henwife put the honey-birds on her shoulders. She placed the hat on her head, clipped a few hairs from one lock and a few hairs from another, and at once clouds of the most beautiful golden hair flowed down over Trembling's shoulders.

"And what kind of a mare would you like?" asked the henwife.

"White," said Trembling, happily, "with blue and gold diamonds all over its body, and a gold saddle and bridle."

The mare stood by the door, with a skylark sitting between her ears. The bird began to sing as soon as Trembling was in the saddle, and never stopped till she came home from church.

The fame of the beautiful lady had gone out through the world, and all the princes and great men came to church that Sunday, each one hoping to take her home with him after Mass. The son of the King of Omanya forgot all about the eldest sister, and stayed outside to catch the strange lady before she hurried away.

As soon as the people were rising up at the end of Mass, Trembling ran to the glittering mare, sprang into the golden saddle, and was away. But the Prince of Omanya was at her side and holding onto her leg. He ran with the mare for thirty strides

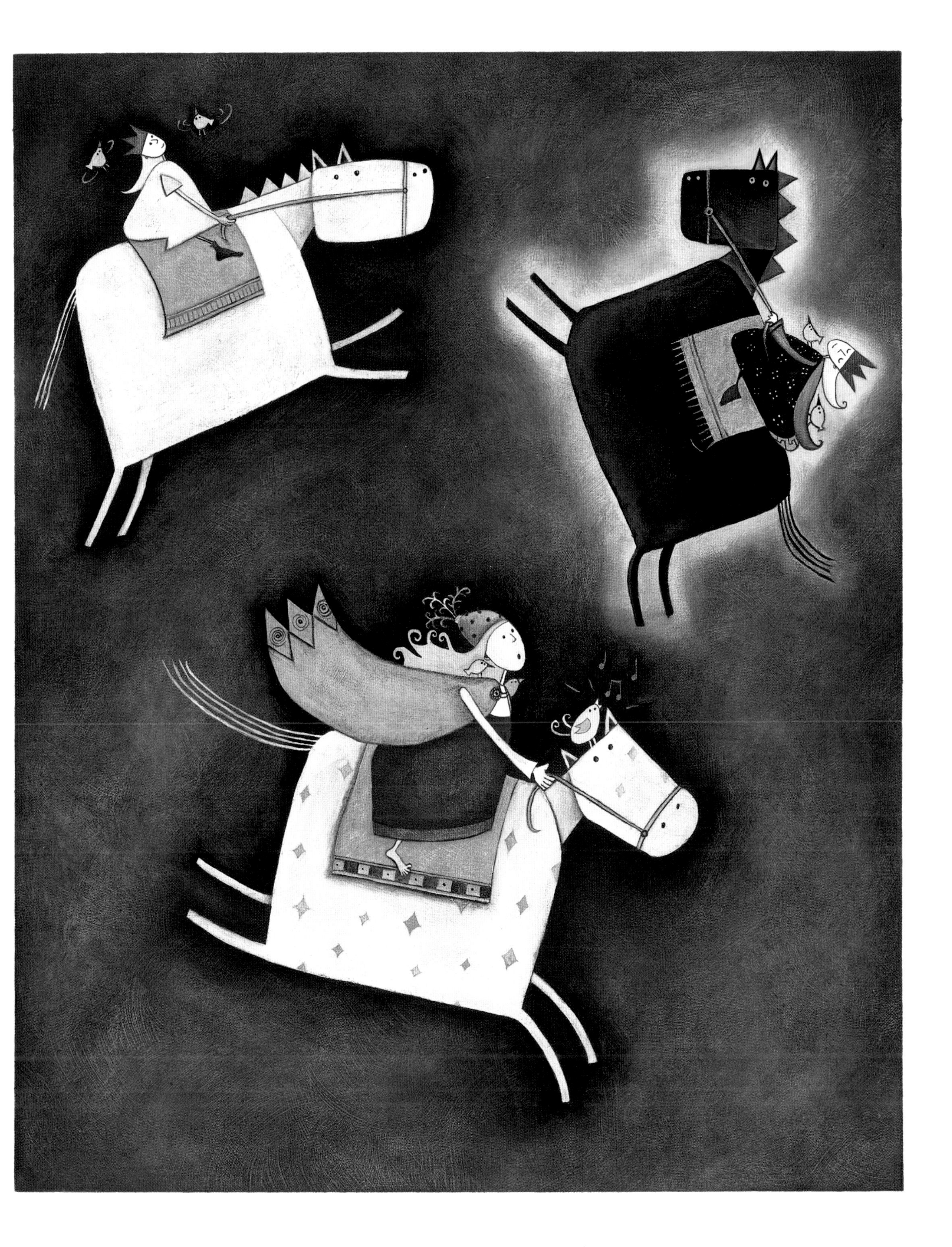

and never let go till the shoe was pulled from Trembling's foot.

"What's the matter, dear?" said the henwife, seeing the girl return with tears streaming down her face.

"I lost one of your pretty shoes, Henny," she sobbed.

"Oh, never mind about that," said the henwife, drying Trembling's tears. "You may be glad of the loss before long."

Trembling gave up her clothes and went to work. When the sisters came in, the henwife asked, "Any news from the church?"

"The worst news possible!" said they. "The strange lady was back, in even richer array than before. On herself and her horse were the finest fabrics of the world, and between the mare's ears was a bird which never stopped singing from the time she arrived to the time she left. She's the most beautiful woman Ireland's ever seen, and nobody takes a blind bit of notice of us any more!"

Well, the son of the King of Omanya was madly in love by now, and it wasn't with the eldest sister.

"I shall have that beautiful lady as my wife if it's the last thing I do!" said he to the other kings' sons.

"You'll need more than the shoe off her foot," said they. "And you'll have to fight for her, as every one of us wants her, too."

"When I find the one whose shoe this is," cried the prince, "I'll fight for her tooth and nail, for she'll marry no one but me!"

So all the kings' sons followed Omanya as he roamed the length and breadth of Ireland to find the lady whose foot would fit the red, white and green shoe. North, south, east and west they went and there wasn't a house in the kingdom they didn't search.

The Prince of Omanya never let the shoe out of his sight, and when the young women saw it they were all of a flutter, for every one of them hoped it would fit them and they'd get

to marry the handsome prince. What with cutting their toes and stuffing their stockings, didn't they do everything they could think of to catch the son of the King of Omanya, but he wouldn't have one of them.

Fair and Brown couldn't wait for all the great men to come calling. Each was determined to make sure the shoe would be seen as theirs, and they never stopped going on about it till Trembling was fed up with their chatter.

"Maybe it's my foot the shoe will fit!" she said one day, and her two sisters rolled about in fits of laughter at the very idea.

"You!" they roared, clutching their sides and guffawing. "You in your tatters and rags, who never sets foot out of the house! There's not much chance they'd think you were the beautiful lady! Shut up and get back to your cleaning!"

At that very moment, the princes rode up to the door, so the sisters shoved Trembling in a wardrobe.

When the company came into the house, the Prince of Omanya gave the shoe to Fair and Brown and, though they tried and tried to put it on, it would fit neither of them.

"Is there any other young woman here?" asked the Prince.

The sisters were just about to say no, when Trembling piped up from the wardrobe.

"There is," she called. "In here!"

"Oh, don't bother with her," said Fair and Brown. "She's just a silly wee thing we keep to put out the ashes."

But the prince wouldn't leave the house till he'd seen her, so the two sisters had to open the door. When Trembling came out, she tried the shoe on her foot, and it fitted exactly.

"You are the woman I love," said the Prince of Omanya, staring deep into her eyes, "and the woman I'll marry. Say you'll be mine."

"I will," said Trembling, for she knew she loved him also. "But wait till I prove who I am."

She ran to the henwife, who dressed her in everything she had worn the first Sunday. Back she came on the white mare, and the people cried, "This is the lady we saw at church."

Trembling returned to the henwife, changed into the clothes she had worn the second Sunday, and rode up on the black mare.

"Yes, this is the lady, for sure," said everyone.

A last time Trembling turned, and came back in the third dress.

"You don't need to prove yourself," said the prince. "I knew you were the woman I loved as soon as I gazed into your eyes."

The sisters were hopping mad, and the other young men were all for drawing their swords and fighting the Prince of Omanya for Trembling's hand. But the henwife appeared and put a spell on them all, so they couldn't speak or move until the brave prince had climbed up behind Trembling and the two of them galloped off into the sunset.

So the son of the King of Omanya married the beautiful Trembling. They had fourteen children, and lived happily till they died of old age in each other's arms.

The Twelve Wild Geese

We're always wishing for what we don't have and not caring for what we've already got, and so it was with the Queen of Leinster long ago. She had twelve sons and not a single daughter, and she was half mad with envy for every little girl she saw.

One day in winter, when the courtyard was covered in snow, the queen was looking out of the window. There, lying on the frozen ground, was a calf, just killed by the butcher, and a raven standing by it.

"Oh," said she, "if only I had a daughter with skin as white as snow, cheeks as red as blood and hair as black as that raven, I'd give all my twelve sons for her."

In that instant, a strange old woman appeared before her.

"That's a wicked thing to say," said the old woman. "To punish you for even thinking it, I shall grant your wish. You will have such a daughter, but the very day she's born, you will lose your other children." And with that, she vanished.

The queen became pregnant, and she could tell from the first day that she carried a girl. She didn't dare tell the king about her wish, but to keep her sons safe, she told him that she feared her thirteenth childbirth, and that she would like all her sons around her to bring her luck when the time came.

So it was that on the day she gave birth the boys were gathered around, with guards at every door. But the very hour her daughter came into the world, the guards heard a great whirling and whistling, and twelve wild geese were seen flying one after another out of the open window and away like arrows through the Great Forest.

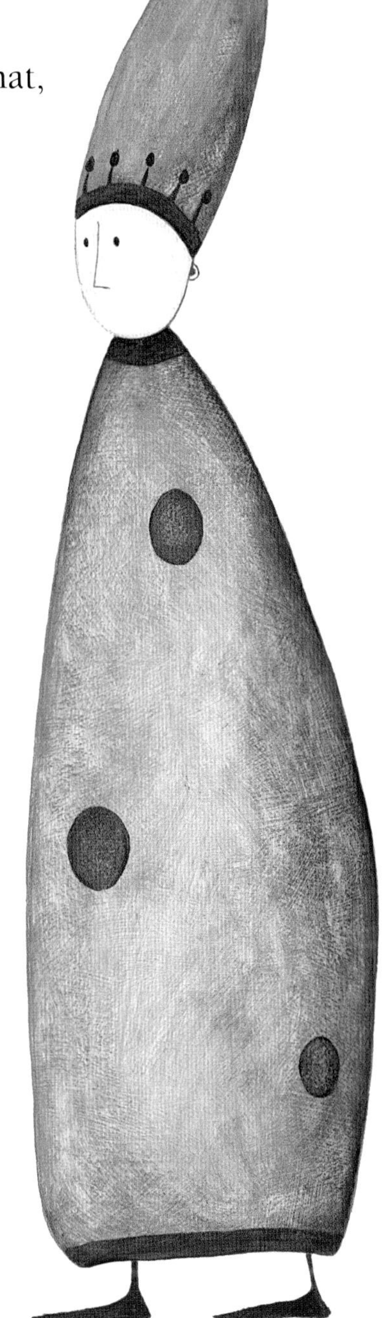

The king was in great grief for the loss of his sons, and there's no telling what he would have done to his wife if he had found out that she was to blame.

For although it was evil that brought her about, there was no trace of evil in the heart of the little princess. Bevin she was called, meaning fair lady, on account of the snowy whiteness of her skin, and she was the most loving and lovable child.

The young princess was happy as could be for the first twelve years of her life, but then she began to wonder why she had no brothers or sisters, and began to feel lonely. She heard it whispered that her brothers were dead, and she tormented her mother with questions about what happened, until the queen gave in and told her.

Bevin took the news badly. “It’s my fault that my brothers became wild geese,” she said. “I shall go and find them, and return them to their former shapes.”

The queen had her closely watched, but it was no use. Bevin slipped out of the palace and was away into the darkness of the Great Forest before the night was done.

On she went, through morning, afternoon and evening, until she came to a small wooden house in a clearing. She went in and saw a table laid for twelve. She saw meat and bread, cakes and fruit, and a blazing fire in the hearth. Through a door, there were twelve beds, and Bevin knew that she had come to the right place.

The gate opened and Bevin heard footsteps on the path. In came twelve young men, and there was sadness on their faces when they laid eyes on her.

“What misfortune sent you here, child?” said the eldest. “For it was because of a girl that we were banished from court and made to live as wild geese. Only in the hours of darkness do we take human form. Twelve long, unhappy years we’ve lived under this curse, and at the height of our anger we swore to get revenge by killing the first young girl who came into our hands!”

“But I’m your only sister,” said Bevin, “and I never knew a thing about you until yesterday. As soon as I heard, I stole away from the palace to find you and see how I could help to relieve you of your curse."

The young men were at a loss what to do, for oaths cannot be broken, until an old woman suddenly appeared among them.

"I permit you to break your wicked oath," said she. "Your sister has come to save you, but it will not be easy. She must spin and knit twelve shirts from bog-down, which she must gather with her own hands. It will take her five years, and if she speaks or laughs or cries in all that time, you shall remain wild geese until the day you die. Take care of young Bevin, for she is your only hope."

With that the fairy vanished, for fairy she was, and the brothers each in turn hugged and kissed their long lost sister.

For the next three years, the princess spent all day every day picking bog-down, spinning it and knitting it into shirts, until she had finished eight. During all that time, she never spoke a word nor laughed nor cried, although the work was hard and heavy.

One fine day, she was sitting in the garden spinning, when a great hound bounded over the gate. Bevin screamed, fearing for her life as its paws reached her shoulders, but it licked her forehead and her hair. The next minute, a handsome young king rode up to the gate, took off his hat, and asked to be allowed to enter. She gave a little nod and in he came.

The king fell in love with Bevin the moment he set eyes on her. He begged her to come back with him to his palace on the far side of the Great Forest, for he wished to make her his queen.

Bevin couldn't help loving the young King of Connacht as much as he loved her, and although she shook her head a thousand times, for she did not want to leave her brothers, a thousand and one times he asked, and at last she nodded her assent. She put her hand in his, allowed him to kiss her on the lips, and then she gathered up her shirts and bog-down and rode away.

As soon as he arrived home, the king sent for his bishop,

and he and Bevin were married. He cared not that Bevin would not speak, for love runs deeper than words.

In good time, the new queen gave birth to a beautiful baby boy and the king's heart was overrun with happiness. But there was a blot on the joy of the court, in the form of the king's wicked stepmother. She was jealous of Bevin, jealous of their love and she determined to put a stop to it.

She followed Bevin to her bedchamber, gave her a sleeping potion and stole the tiny baby from her side. Taking him to the window, she saw a hungry wolf below and tossed him down. The beast caught the boy in its jaws and was over the fence and away before anyone could see. The wicked woman pricked her finger, dabbed the blood around the mouth of the sleeping mother and away she fled to fetch the king.

"What have you done with our son?" cried he, when he saw Bevin's bloody mouth.

But despite the queen's grief, she could not answer, for she knew that if she did, her brothers would never be human again.

"What have you done, I said?" the king shouted, shaking her.

His wife neither spoke nor shed a tear.

"She has always been strange," his stepmother whispered in the king's ear. "You should never have married her."

Try as he did to find some other explanation, the king could not, and at last he came to believe that his beloved queen had devoured her own son. He was wild with sorrow, and it took all the strength of the guards to stop him from destroying Bevin in his rage.

When at last the king was calmer, he resolved not to punish his wife too harshly, for he understood that she must have been mad to do such a terrible thing, and he could not blame her for an act of madness. He could not hate her either, for she had given him a beautiful child, one whom he had loved dearly. He decided to allow her to remain in the palace, at least until she had a second child, but to keep the child always under the closest guard.

He told his stepmother to spread the word that by a cruel twist of fate the child had fallen from a window into the jaws of a wild beast. But the wicked woman hinted to one and all of the blood on the queen's lips, until everyone believed poor Bevin to be a witch.

Bevin knew that her husband was only keeping her until she had another child. She knew that all the people in the land hated her and yet she could not tell the truth, for she could not utter a word until she had finished the last of the twelve shirts. So she hid away in the tower, gathering bog-down by moonlight when no one could see her, and making her shirts.

The only joy she had in those long dark months was when the twelve wild geese would come to the trees in the park and look in at her window. She knew they loved her, and that in time she would bring them back to human form and then be able to tell her husband and her people the truth of what had happened.

At last another year was at an end, and she had the twelfth shirt finished except for one arm, when she took to her bed, and a beautiful girl was born.

The king would not allow mother and child to be alone together for a second. But the wicked stepmother bribed some of the guards to let her take their place. She gave a sleeping potion to the queen and tossed the child from the window, into the jaws of the wolf, who again was waiting below.

Again she pricked her finger, again she smeared the queen's mouth with blood, and again his stepmother told the king and everyone she met that the queen had devoured her own child.

Poor Bevin was distraught, and thought her life must leave her. The king, whose grief was more than he could bear, gave up on her and she was thrown into the deepest dungeon, with only her knitting. She could neither think nor pray, but sat like a stone, working away at the arm of the twelfth shirt.

The king, when he had recovered slightly, was all for taking Bevin back to the little house in the wood where he'd found her, for she had brought him nothing but bad luck and he wished to turn time back to the days before he'd met her. But his stepmother and the lords of court would not hear of it, and Bevin was condemned to be burned in the courtyard at three o'clock.

As the hour drew near, the king went to the farthest part of his palace, and there was no sadder man in the land.

When the guards came and led Bevin up to the courtyard, she took the pile of shirts in her arms. There were still a few stitches needed, and desperately she worked them, even while she was tied to the stake. At the last stitch, she was overcome with grief. A tear dropped on her work, but the job was done.

"I am innocent!" she called out. "Fetch my husband!"

The executioners stayed their hands, except for one who was so surprised to hear her shout that he dropped his burning torch. The woodpile went up in flames, but in a rushing of wings the twelve wild geese were standing next to Bevin. In an instant, she flung a shirt over each bird, and there stood twelve fine young men.

They untied their sister and pulled her from the flames. While they were comforting the young queen, and the king was hurrying to the spot, an old woman appeared among the crowd, holding a tiny princess on one arm and a little prince on the other.

There was crying and laughing, hugging and kissing, and no one recognized the old woman, the fairy woman, who had twice become a wolf in order to save the prince and princess.

The wicked stepmother was put to death in Bevin's place, and everyone lived in comfort for the rest of their lives.

Lusmore and the Fairies

There was a poor man living in the green glen of Aherlow, at the foot of the Galtee Mountains, and he had a hump on his back the size of a football. Lusmore, as he was known, for he always wore a sprig of foxglove in his hat, looked as if his body had been rolled up and put on his shoulders. When he sat down, the hump was so heavy that it pushed his head all the way to his knees.

The country people were shy of meeting him alone, for although he was harmless, evil folk had put out strange stories about him. Some said he was a changeling, a child of the fairies, and others said he must be in league with the Devil, which was a terrible lie, for you'd have to cross seven counties to meet a kinder man.

Lusmore spent his days sitting on a stool at his cottage door, braiding rushes into hats and baskets. He was an expert at his trade, and could get more for his work than anyone else in the land.

He lived on his own on the edge of the village of Cappagh, and one morning he was up before dawn to take his hats and baskets to the market in Cahir. He had a good day and sold every one, but he was weary going home, and his hump was weighing heavy on his back. It was dark by the time he reached the old mound of Knock-grafton, so, although he still had a great distance to travel, poor old Lusmore sat down to rest. He was almost dropping off to sleep, when what should he hear but the strangest song:

Monday, Tuesday; Monday, Tuesday; Monday, Tuesday…

That's how it went, before stopping a second or two and beginning again. Lusmore thought he'd never heard such sweet, high-pitched singing. It was like the sound of many tiny voices, all blending in with one another, and he listened closely, scarcely drawing his breath.

He looked all around to try and work out where the sound was coming from, and realized to his amazement that it couldn't be from anywhere but inside the mound. Pressing his ear to the grass, he listened even more closely to the sweet sounds. But after a while, the music, which had at first seemed so beautiful, began to bore him. Lusmore started to think it was a shame that the only thing the fairies sang was Monday, Tuesday, over and over. It was as though they didn't know what was supposed to follow.

So the next time they paused at the end of their round, Lusmore took up the tune himself and added a bit in the silence:

Monday, Tuesday; Monday, Tuesday; Monday, Tuesday, Wednesday!

The fairies of Knockgrafton, for they were the singers, were delighted when they heard Lusmore's addition to their tune, and listened while he sang the whole thing through.

"Why didn't we think of that before?" said the king of the fairies, appearing before him. "It's perfect. And who are you that's brought us such a gift?"

"I'm Lusmore," he said, in awe, for he'd never spoken to a fairy before. "And I'm very glad you liked my words. I'd be delighted to have you take them up, for you sing so beautifully."

"Well, you're a great man for the music, Lusmore," said the king. "More skilled than any of us. Would you come down to meet the rest of my people, for I'm sure they'd all like to thank you for themselves?"

"There's nothing would give me greater pleasure," said the hunchback.

He followed the king of the fairies along a dark tunnel that led into the hill, until they arrived at a magnificent palace. The fairies gave him a hearty welcome and asked him to sing the song through again. They danced around him, listening and then singing, till they were sure they had mastered it. Then they invited him to sit at the head of the table, next to the king, for they were about to have a great feast.

When they had finished their banquet, Lusmore joined in the dancing until the fairy king called for a halt to the music and stepped up to him, saying:

Lusmore, Lusmore,

The hump which you bore

On your back is no more.

Look down on the floor,

Lusmore!

The man looked to the ground, and saw the hump tumble from his shoulders! Lusmore straightened his back, for the very first time in his life, only to find he was so tall that his head scraped the ceiling of the grand hall. As he looked around, the joy and the beauty made him dizzy, his eyesight grew dim, and he fell into a deep sleep.

He awoke to broad daylight. The sun was shining, the birds were singing, and he found himself at the foot of the mound of Knockgrafton, with the cows and sheep grazing all around.

The first thing Lusmore did was to feel for his hump, to see if he'd only been dreaming. But sure enough, it was gone. He stood up and stretched, and wasn't it wonderful to feel his back straightening and to be able to hold his head up to the sky, tall and proud! He looked himself up and down and saw a well-shaped, dapper sort

of a fellow, in a brand new suit that the fairies had made for him.

He stepped out lightly to return to Cappagh, with a new found spring in his step. No one he met along the way recognized him, and he was hard-pressed to convince them that he was old Lusmore, the basket maker.

It wasn't long before his story got out, though, and a great fuss was made of him by young and old. One morning, he was sitting contentedly at the door of his cottage when an old woman came up to him, asking the way to Cappagh.

"Sure you're there already," said he. "Who are you looking for?"

"I've come all the way from Waterford looking for a man called Lusmore," said she, "who I hear tell had his hump removed by the fairies. There's a son of mine has a hump also, and I want to find out the charm so he can get rid of it."

"I'm the man you're after," said Lusmore, and being a good-natured fellow, he told her all that had happened — how he'd

raised the tune for the little people, how his hump had been taken from his shoulders, and how he'd got a new suit of clothes into the bargain.

The woman thanked him and hurried home to fetch her son. But Jack Madden, for that was his name, wasn't a bit like Lusmore. Nasty people take all shapes and forms, from fat to thin, from ugly to beautiful, and this particular fellow was one of the worst. The woman put her son on a cart, for he was too lazy to walk, and pushed him to Knockgrafton. The grumpy man complained every inch of the way. His mother left him sitting on the grassy mound and went off to spend the night in Cahir.

Jack Madden hadn't been there long when he heard the tune coming from the fairy hill. And if Lusmore had heard sweet music, the tune Jack Madden heard was ten times sweeter. For instead of stopping at Monday, Tuesday, it carried on, round and round and ever rounder, thanks to Lusmore's help.

Monday, Tuesday; Monday, Tuesday; Monday, Tuesday, Wednesday;

Monday, Tuesday; Monday, Tuesday; Monday, Tuesday, Wednesday;

But Jack Madden had no ear for a tune. All he wanted was to get rid of his hump, and his mother had told him how to do it. So he never thought to listen to the music to see if he could improve on it. Instead, having heard the fairies sing it over seven times without stopping, out he bawled, never heeding the tune.

"*Thursday and Friday*!" he screeched, at the top of his voice, thinking that if one day was good, two days were better, and he might even get an extra suit of clothes into the bargain.

No sooner had the words passed his lips than he was whisked into the hill with prodigious force, and the fairies were all around him in great anger.

"What's that horrible noise?" they screamed.

"Who spoiled our tune?" they roared. And the fairy king stepped up to him and said:

Jack Madden! Jack Madden!

Your words are so bad in

The tune we feel glad in;

Your life we will sadden —

Two humps for Jack Madden!

And twenty of the strongest fairies came up carrying Lusmore's hump and pressed it down on Jack Madden's back, where it stayed for the rest of his days.

They put Jack Madden out of their castle into the pitch dark night and, in the morning, his mother found him at the foot of the mound, with a hump twice the size it was the day before.

"What happened, Jack?" she asked, but he wouldn't tell, for fear the little people might put a third hump on his back. She put him in the cart and wheeled him home to Waterford.

Everyone said that's the sort of thing that happens if you don't pay proper respect to the fairies. And they're right.

Son of an Otter, Son of a Wolf

Long ago, there was a King of Ireland named Cormac, who ruled wisely and well. One summer, he decided to make a tour of the island, spending a while in each of his palaces. His wife went with him, but his three beautiful daughters asked to stay behind, to enjoy the warm weather at home.

While the cat's away the mice will play, and so it was with the daughters. There was a big lake below the palace, and nothing would satisfy them but to go swimming there, although they had often been warned not to.

While they were in the middle of the lake one day, a great otter raised his head. The girls made for the shore as fast as they could, but the otter overtook the youngest and swam alongside her.

When the day came for King Cormac to return, his daughters stepped out to meet him. But when the youngest went to kiss her father, he drew back.

"Get out of my sight, girl!" he shouted. "Three months ago when I left you, there was a maiden's look in your eye, but now I see that you are with child!"

Crying and moaning, the girl told her father what had happened with the otter.

"I believe you," said the king, at last. "It could not have been avoided, and it may all turn out for the best."

Time went by and the girl gave birth to a fine young boy. The old king was delighted, for his only son had died many years before. He called the boy Lorcan, and he carried him on his shoulders everywhere he went. The boy was given all that he asked for, and he grew strong and healthy, but spoiled.

One day, when Lorcan was eight years old, he was walking along the lake shore with the king, when Cormac complained that he felt tired.

"You are growing old, Father," said Lorcan, for he only knew the king as his father. "Perhaps it would be better to hand your crown over to me. I could look after everything for you, and I'd be happy to let you stay in the palace."

"Bide your time, boy," said the king, gently. "You will rule the country soon enough."

A while later they were out again together, and, at the end of the day, the king complained of aches and pains.

"Let me be king," said Lorcan. "Then you can rest at home."

"I shall not do so while I live," said Cormac. "But you are like a son to me, Lorcan. Wait patiently, and you shall take my place in due course."

At that the boy became angry. "I want the crown and I want it now!" he yelled. "If you don't give me it willingly, old man, I shall take it by force!"

He left the king, stomped off down the road, and in the late evening, he came to the house of Fionn Mac Cumhail, the leader of the Fianna.

"Fionn Mac Cumhail," said Lorcan, for he feared no one, "I will work for you for a year and a day, and if you find any fault with me, you may pay me what you wish. But if you find no fault, I shall choose my own reward."

"It's a deal," said Fionn, shaking his hand, thinking he would surely find some fault in the boy over the course of a year.

Lorcan did everything he was asked. No matter what task he set the lad, Fionn could find no fault with him. When the year and a day were up, he called Lorcan and said, "I will pay you as we agreed. What do you choose as your reward?"

"All I ask is for you to fight King Cormac," replied Lorcan, "for I want his crown."

"My very own king!" cried Fionn. "How could I fight him?" But he had made the deal, and he had to stick to it.

Now, while Lorcan had been away, King Cormac's wife had died. The king no longer wanted to leave his throne to Lorcan, and he hoped that by remarrying he might provide a son and heir. He had taken a fancy to the youngest daughter of the blacksmith, and when he heard that Lorcan and Fionn were preparing to fight him, he married her within the week.

"You had better go home to your father," the king told his new wife. "I might be killed in this battle and who knows what will happen then." He told her where he had hidden a basket of gold and silver and he gave her a belt, on which he had inscribed "Aidan, son of Cormac."

"If God sends you a son, and I pray that he will, put this belt on him. When he is old enough to read, he will know who his father was, and he will claim his rights from the thief who is coming to take his place."

The hour of the battle arrived. It was a day of great bloodshed and many were killed, including King Cormac. The lords of the land met to see what was to be done, and decided that, despite what had happened, Lorcan was lawful heir to the throne, for Cormac had always considered him his son.

And so it was that the Son of an Otter came to rule Ireland.

Lorcan was a very different sort of a king from Cormac, and soon everyone hated him. The wind changed to the north, the land refused to yield crops and the people were hungry. Lorcan would not help them, and, if they fell behind with their rent, he threw them into prison.

In time, the smith's daughter gave birth to King Cormac's son. She hid in a wood, for fear of the new king, and she put the belt

Cormac had given her around the infant. No sooner had she done so than, to her horror, a she-wolf appeared. The creature picked the boy up in her mouth and ran off, and the poor woman had no chance of saving him.

The wolf carried the child to her cave, licked him to keep him warm and suckled him alongside her own three cubs. The child was happy enough with the wolves. He lived with them for a year, and, on fine days, they would leave the cave and play together.

One day, some hunters happened to pass close by and caught sight of the wolf lying on her back on the grass, playing with the child and the cubs. The wolves smelled the men and flew to their hidden cave, but the hunters caught the child.

The boy scratched and scraped them, but they were determined to hold onto him. They brought him to an old nobleman who

lived close by. The nobleman and his wife had never had children, and were overjoyed to be given the child, wild as he was. They called him Aidan, for that was the name on his belt, and brought him up as their own. They never thought that he might be the son of a king, for Cormac was a common name in those times.

The old couple looked after him well, and in time Aidan grew bigger and stronger than all the other boys in the parish. The son of one of the men who had found him overheard his father talking and, taking a dislike to Aidan, for he didn't like to be beaten by him in games, called him Son of the Wolf.

Aidan went home that night and asked his parents why the other children were laughing at him and calling him such a name.

"You were found in the woods with a wolf and three cubs," said the nobleman. "The hunters left you here to bring us joy and to be heir to my lands."

"Had I nothing to tell where I came from?" asked Aidan.

"You were naked as the day you were born," said the woman, "except for a belt tied around your waist."

"Show it to me," Aidan said.

So the nobleman fetched the belt and gave it to the boy.

"Aidan, son of Cormac," he read. "I'm no son of a wolf! I'm the son of King Cormac himself, and I'm going to claim his lands!"

"Oh, Aidan," said the nobleman, "just because your father was called Cormac doesn't mean he was the old king!"

But the boy wouldn't listen. The nobleman and his wife warned him that it would be madness to challenge the cruel Lorcan, but he would have none of it.

"I'm not your true son and you can't stop me," he said. "I know well enough how to look after myself."

So the next morning, with a good meal in his belly and their sad farewells ringing in his ears, he took to the road.

By evening, he came to a small house. He saw an old man herding his sheep, and little did he know it was the blacksmith, his own true grandfather!

"Hello, sir," said Aidan. "Have you any idea where King Cormac used to live?"

"Over there," said the old man, pointing to a fine palace, "though he's dead these fifteen years.

A thief who hasn't given us peace day or night has stolen his crown. The weather's bad and the crops are worse, and the new king has made a law that if these three little sheep of mine go onto his land, he'll keep them."

"He sounds like a cruel man to have as a king," said the boy.

The man invited Aidan to stay the night. The boy had eaten his fill and was stretched out in his chair, nodding off, when he heard a noise, and there was the youngest of the smith's three daughters, staring at his belt.

"What are you looking at?" he asked. "And why are you crying?"

"I married King Cormac just before he was killed," sobbed the woman. "He gave me that belt and told me if I had a child to put it on him, so that he would know who his father was. A wolf took my sweet boy, and I've never had trace nor tidings of him since."

"Then you are my mother," cried Aidan, "and I am home!"

The woman was delighted, and she threw her arms around him. "Come quick, everyone," she called. "I've found my long lost son, the child of King Cormac!"

The family stayed up late, drinking whiskey and celebrating. During the night, the talk turned to the wicked king, and how someone had to sit up every night telling him stories. If they didn't satisfy him, they were hanged in the morning.

"Run out and check the sheep," said the old man to one of his daughters at first light. Soon she was back, with the news that there was a hole in the wall, and no sign of the sheep.

"What will I do now?" cried the old man. "The king will hold onto them and they're my only wealth in the world."

"I'll tell you what," said Aidan. "Go up there and plead with him. If he won't give them back, ask him to leave the decision about who should keep them to the first man who comes along."

So the old man went up and begged the king for his sheep, but Lorcan would not listen.

"I checked the whole length of that wall only yesterday," said the smith. "One of your soldiers must have pulled it down on purpose. How about if we leave it to the first man that comes along this road to decide what is just?"

"All right," said the king, for he knew that no one in their right mind would have the courage to oppose his laws.

They waited and waited, and along came King Cormac's son.

"Hold there, stranger!" said the king, and told him of the law and how he planned to keep the three sheep. "What do you say now, isn't it only fair and just to uphold the law?"

"We should all keep to the law," said the boy, "when the law is fair, but I'm not so sure about this one. Why don't you shear the sheep instead, and keep the wool in return for the grass they ate?"

The king scowled, but he had to keep to his word, so he agreed. Two days later, he summoned the old man to tell him stories all night.

"This is his revenge," said the blacksmith, sadly. "He'll kill me for sure."

"I'll go instead," said Aidan. "I have plenty of stories for him."

"No!" cried the old man. "You are too young to die."

"He won't kill me as easily as you think," said the boy, thrusting his sword into his scabbard. "Take your ease and stay at home."

"I've come to tell you stories," said Aidan, when he was brought to the king's room. "The old blacksmith was taken ill."

"Very well," said Lorcan, stretched out on a bed of birds' down by the fire. "But you'd better be good!" He turned his face to the

liom
Rí
leaba a chodladh
Scéalta
oíche
dul a
oíche
Rí
chodladh
mo

wall, with the sheets drawn up over his head, and the boy began. When dawn was breaking the next morning, the king turned to face him. "Not bad," said he.

"Thank you," said Aidan, "but I don't believe you heard the half of what I told you, for you were sleeping most of the night."

"I was not!" said the king. "I haven't closed my eyes in sleep these seven years at least."

"Then," said the youth, "you must be half an otter, for they're the only creatures I know that never sleep."

The king's face turned red with anger. "Don't say that again, boy," he cried, "or it'll be the last thing you say!"

"If your mother's alive," said Aidan, "go and ask her."

The king went out of the room and came back in a few minutes.

"She says I came from King Cormac," he said, triumphantly. "He's my father!"

The king asked Aidan to come back again the next night and, as before, he covered his head while the boy went on with his stories. In the morning, the king praised Aidan again for his storytelling, and Aidan replied that he couldn't have heard the half of it, for he'd been asleep.

"I heard every word!" said the king.

"Then you must be half an otter, as I told you before."

"I warned you not to say that again!" cried the king, reaching for his sword.

"I have a sword, too!" cried the boy, drawing first and holding the point to the king's throat.

"Don't kill me!" cried the king, desperately. "I'll give you anything you want."

"Go back to your mother," ordered Aidan, "and tell her you must know the truth about your father!"

So Lorcan went to his mother, with Aidan by his side, and the king told her she must be truthful or the boy would kill him.

The old woman told Lorcan about the day that she and her sisters were bathing and how the otter came to her. "The boy's right," she finished, sadly. "You are no son of King Cormac."

"I always knew there was something strange about me," said Lorcan, slowly. "I can never sleep and yet I need to sleep. My tiredness puts me in such awful rages that I do the cruellest things."

"I know," said the old woman, quietly. "I've always been afraid to tell you where you came from, for fear of your anger."

Up spoke Aidan. "Before another week is out, I could give you the power of sleep, King Lorcan."

"That is what I wish for more than anything," said the king. "If you can help me sleep, I will give you half my possessions and the crown after my death."

"It's a deal," said the boy, and he persuaded the king to put it in writing. "Have you any good boats?"

"Plenty," said the king.

"Fetch one and bring it here," said the boy. "Anchor it in the middle of the lake, make your bed on deck and I promise that you will sleep."

And so it was done. The boat was brought, a bed of

birds' down was made up on the open deck, and King Lorcan lay down to sleep. Three days and three nights he slept, and he never woke.

And what was in the lake but his father! The great otter caught the smell of his long lost son, came up in the night and dragged King Lorcan down to the very bottom of the lake. When the servants went to check the king the next morning, they could find no trace of him.

"The king has disappeared," they said, and only Aidan knew where he had gone. He went to the lords of the land and showed them the letter that King Lorcan had written, passing the crown to him in the event of his death. And in time they agreed that since the king was gone, and as he had no son and heir, the boy could be king in his place.

Aidan sent for the nobleman and his wife to come and end their days with him. He invited his grandfather, his mother and her sisters as well. Then he put out an invitation to the four quarters of his kingdom. Rich and poor gathered, festivities took place as had never been seen in Ireland before, and the people were overjoyed that a new young king was ruling over them.

And that's how Son of a Wolf replaced Son of an Otter as King of all Ireland.

The Soul Cages

Jack Doherty was a fisherman. He lived in Dunbeg Bay, on the coast of County Clare, with his wife, Biddy, in the house that his father and grandfather had lived in before him. People used to wonder why the Dohertys stayed there, among the huge shattered rocks, with only the seals and the seagulls for company, but they had their reasons.

The cottage was sheltered, and there was a neat little inlet close by, where a boat could lie snug as a puffin in a nest. But a ledge of sunken rocks ran out to sea. On cold winter nights, when a westerly wind drove the Atlantic Ocean onto the coast, many a ship went to pieces out on those rocks.

The riches that washed ashore! Fine bales of cotton and

tobacco, barrels of wine and puncheons of rum, casks of brandy and kegs of gin. You can see why Dunbeg Bay was a good enough place for the Dohertys.

Not that Jack and Biddy didn't do their best for any poor sailor that made it to land. More than once Jack put out in his little curragh, breasting the billows like a gannet, to lend a hand to bring the men from a wreck. But when the ship was gone to pieces and the crew was all lost, who could blame Jack for collecting what he found?

So they lived a comfortable enough life, what with a constant supply of fish, and everything they needed from trading with the richest houses in Ireland. But there was one thing Jack wanted more than anything else, and that was to meet a Merrow.

Now, Merrows are the men who live under the sea, and it is said that if you meet one, it will bring you great luck. The coast of County Clare, and the waters around Dunbeg Bay in particular, were full of them, and often Jack thought he had seen one in the mist, moving along the face of the water, but it was always gone by the time he got close. It annoyed Jack that his grandfather had met them often, yet he had never caught a clear view of one himself.

But if you try anything for long enough, the chances are you will manage it at last, and so it was with Jack. One day, when he had strolled a little further than usual along the coast to the north, he spotted a Merrow. It was perched on a rock a little way out to sea, with a cocked hat in its hand. Jack stood for a good half hour straining his eyes, and all the time the creature didn't stir hand or foot. At last, Jack decided to make it move, and he gave a loud whistle. The Merrow, for that's what he was, to be sure, jumped up, put the cocked hat on his head and dived from the rock.

Every fine day from then on Jack walked to the point to see if he could catch another glimpse of the thing. But he never did, and soon he came to thinking it must have been a dream. One very rough day though, when the sea was running mountains high, Jack decided to take one more look at the Merrow's rock and there he saw him, diving down and up and down again.

From that day on, Jack knew the time to go — days when the winds were blowing a gale. But it wasn't enough just to see the Merrow, for Jack was determined to get to know him. One blustery day, he was heading down to the point when the rain got so bad that he had to take shelter in a cave. There, to his astonishment, sitting before him was a big fellow with green hair, long dark teeth, a red nose and piggy eyes. He had a fish's tail, legs with scales on them and short arms with fins. He seemed to be thinking deeply.

"It's now or never," thought Jack, so up he went to the Merrow, took off his hat and bowed. "Your servant, sir," he said.

"Your servant kindly, Jack Doherty," answered the Merrow.

"How is it you know my name?" asked Jack, surprised.

"And why wouldn't I?" answered the Merrow, with a merry twinkle in his eye. "Sure your grandfather and I were like two brothers together. A great man he was for drinking, and I never met his match for sucking in a shellful of brandy. Are you any good at it yourself, Jack?"

"Well, I wouldn't know if I'm his equal, but I'm mighty fond of the stuff, to be sure," said Jack. "I suppose you have to drink a power of it down below to keep the heat inside you. Where do you get it from?"

"Same place as you, Jack Doherty," said the Merrow, with a knowing look.

"What sort do you have, then?" asked Jack. "I bet it's not half as good as mine."

"Oh, don't be so sure," answered the Merrow. "Meet me here next Monday and I'll show you."

Jack could think of nothing else for the whole week but meeting up with the creature again and having a sup of his brandy. On the Monday they met, and Jack was surprised to see that the old fellow had two cocked hats with him, one under each arm.

"Why have you two hats?" asked Jack. "Are you giving me one, or what?"

"Indeed and I'm not," said the Merrow. "I'm hoping you'll come down and dine with me in my fine house at the bottom of the sea."

“Bless us and save us!” said Jack. “To the bottom of the salt sea ocean? Sure I’d be choked with the water, to say nothing of being drowned! And what would poor Biddy do then?”

“Stop your complaining, Jack Doherty,” said the Merrow. “Many’s the time your grandfather put that same hat on his head and dived down boldly after me. And many’s the fine dinner and shellful of brandy he and I had there. Are you coming or not, for it’s the only time I’ll ask you?”

“I’ll be no worse a man than my grandfather,” said Jack, finding his courage at last. “Lead the way, sir!”

They left the cave and swam to the rock, where they climbed up out of the water.

“Put this hat on your head,” said the Merrow. “Take a hold of my tail and you’ll see what you’ll see.”

In he dashed, and in dashed Jack after him. Down and down they went, till Jack thought they’d never reach the bottom. It was terribly wet and ferociously cold, and Jack was wishing he was safe and warm at home by the fire, rather than miles below the Atlantic Ocean. But he held hard to the Merrow’s tail, slippery as it was, and at last, much to his surprise, found himself on a dry sandy plain at the bottom of the sea, outside a fine house, neatly roofed with oyster shells.

"Welcome to my home," said the Merrow.

Jack could hardly speak, out of breath as he was from moving so fast through the water, never mind the wonder. He looked about him and all he could see were great weeds growing out of the sand like trees, and crabs and lobsters walking about. Overhead was the sea for a sky, and fishes like birds swimming about in it.

"I'm neither choked nor drowned!" said Jack with a grin, when he'd got his breath back. "Who in the world would have thought of finding such a fine place all the way down here?"

"Sure, what did I tell you, Jack Doherty?" said the Merrow. "Now, come inside and we'll see what there is to eat."

Into the house they went. There was a big kitchen, a young

Merrow cooking up a meal, and a warm fire blazing in the hearth.

"Come on, and I'll show you where I keep the brandy," said the Merrow. Opening a little door, he led Jack into a fine cellar, well stocked with kegs, hogsheads and barrels. They chose what they wanted to drink and went back to the room to find dinner laid. The choicest of fish they had that day, turbot and sturgeon, lobster and sole, oysters and herring.

Jack ate and drank until he could fit no more in. Then, taking up a last shell of brandy, he said, "Here's health to you, good sir. But isn't it odd that I still don't know your name?"

"Coomara," replied the old man, "that's me. But you can call me Coo."

"May you live in good health these fifty years and more, Coo," said Jack, raising his shell.

"Fifty years!" said the Merrow, laughing. "Sure haven't I lived five hundred already! Now follow me and I'll show you my curiosities!"

He opened a little door and led his guest into another room, where Jack saw a great many odds and ends that Coomara had picked up at one time or another. But the thing that puzzled him most were rows of wooden cages all along the wall, like strange-looking lobster pots.

"What are those?" said he to the man.

"Oh, they're my Soul Cages," said Coomara.

"Your what?" said Jack, thinking he hadn't heard properly.

"My Soul Cages," said the old fellow, "where I keep all the souls I find."

"Souls of what?" asked Jack, a chill running down his backbone. "Surely fish don't have souls?"

"Indeed and they don't," said Coomara, coolly. "Sure these are the souls of drowned sailors."

"Bless us and save us!" said Jack. "How did you get them?"

"Easy enough," replied the Merrow. "When I see a good storm coming on, I set out a dozen or so of my pots. Then, when the sailors are drowned and their souls come out of their bodies, they make for my pots. I round them up and keep them here in my house. And now it's about time you were off home, Jack Doherty."

Out they went, and Coomara put one of the cocked hats on Jack's head, the wrong way around, as was right.

"You'll come up just in the same spot you went down in," said Coo. "Be sure and throw me back my hat."

He lifted Jack on his shoulder, launched him into the water and up he shot like a bubble. When he came to the rock he had jumped off, Jack threw in the hat and it sank like a stone.

It was coming on night, so off Jack went home. He didn't say a word to Biddy of where he'd spent the day. But he was deeply troubled by the fate of the poor souls cooped up in the lobster pots, and he set his mind to release them.

Jack knew that Coomara was a good sort of a fellow, but he clearly didn't understand about souls and how they have to be allowed to wander free, so it would be no good reasoning with him. The only thing for it, he decided, was to ask Coo to dinner, to make him drunk, borrow the cocked hat, nip down and open the pots.

So one day when Biddy had gone to visit her sister in Ennis, Jack went to the rock and gave the sign he'd agreed with Coomara, by throwing a big stone into the water. As soon as the ripples had settled, up sprang Coo.

"Good morning, Jack," said he. "How are you keeping?"

"Not so badly," said Jack. "The woman of the house is away. Would you come and join me for a bite of dinner at one o'clock?"

"That'd be great," said Coomara. "I'll see you then."

Jack went home, made up a grand fish dinner and got out the best of his foreign spirits, enough to make twenty men drunk. At the stroke of one, in came Coo, with his cocked hat under his arm, and they sat down to eat.

Jack, thinking of the poor souls below in the pots, plied old Coo with brandy, hoping to drink him under the table. But it was Jack that got drunk, for this time he hadn't the sea over his head to keep him cool, and soon enough Coo reeled off home, leaving Jack as dumb as a haddock on Good Friday.

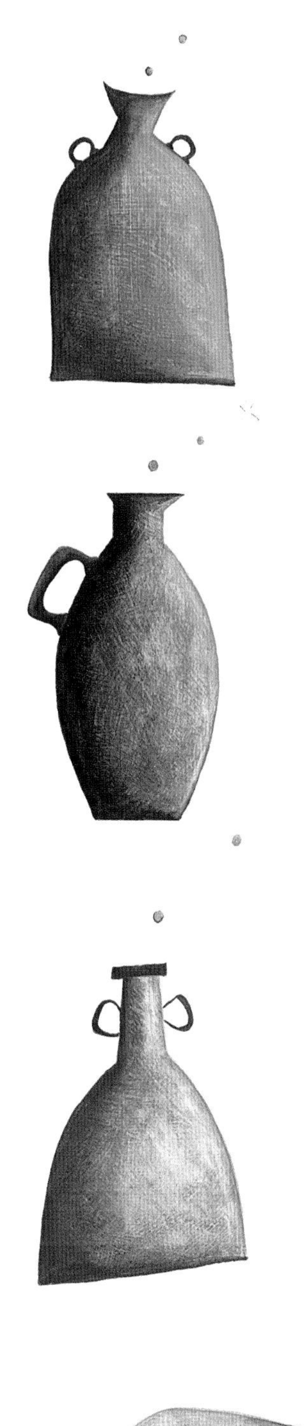

Jack woke the next morning with a pounding head, and racked his brains to find a way to outwit the old Merrow.

"I've got it," he said to himself, after he'd been out for a walk along the cliff tops to clear his head. "I bet he's never touched a drop of poteen, for they never have it on the ships. That'll be the thing to send him to sleep."

So Jack called up Coo again, and the Merrow laughed at him for not being able to hold his drink like his grandfather.

"Try me again," said Jack. "This time I'll drink you drunk and sober."

"Fair enough," said Coo.

Jack took care to have his own drink well watered, and he gave the strongest brandy to Coo. At last he said, "Pray sir, did you ever drink any poteen, that they call the mountain dew?"

"I never did," said Coo. "What's it like and where's it from?"

"Oh, I can't tell you where it's from," said Jack, smiling, "for that's a secret, but it's fifty times as good as brandy or rum. Will you have a drop?"

It was first rate poteen, with the smack of a hammer to it. Coo was delighted. He drank and he sang and he sang and he drank till he fell to the floor in a heap. Jack, who had taken good care to stay sober, snapped up the cocked hat, ran to the rock and was soon at Coo's underwater dwelling.

All was as still as a churchyard at midnight. There was no sign of a Merrow, old or young, so in Jack went and turned over the Soul Cages. He didn't see a thing, but he heard a sort of a little chirp as he lifted each cage. Then he set the pots back as they were before, and sent a blessing after the poor souls to help them on their way.

Jack put on the hat the wrong way, as was right, but when he got out of the house he found the water so high over his head that he wasn't able to get into it. He couldn't find a ladder or a rock, but at last a big cod happened to put down its tail. Jack made a jump and caught hold of it, and the surprised fish gave a bounce and pulled him up. As soon as the hat touched the water, up Jack shot like a cork. He got to the rock in no time and hurried home, rejoicing in the good deed he had done.

Meanwhile, there was a fine fuss at home, for no sooner

had Jack left to open up the Soul Cages, than Biddy had returned from her sister's. She saw the dirty dishes all over the house, the empty bottle of poteen on its side and she was all for yelling and screaming at Jack for getting drunk and leaving the place in such a mess when she heard a terrible grunt from under the table. Looking down, she saw Coomara.

"Jesus, Mary, and Joseph protect me," said she. "My husband's turned himself into a right beast in my absence!"

She rushed out of the house and was running around like a mad thing when she heard the sound of Jack coming along the way, singing a merry tune.

"Oh my Jack, my Jack!" she cried, flinging her arms around him. "I thought you'd turned into some sort of a wild creature!"

Jack knew what had happened, of course, and he told her the whole story. And though she had half a mind to be angry with him for not telling her before, she couldn't, for she was proud of the great service he'd done the poor souls.

Back they went to the house and Jack woke up Coomara. The Merrow had too much of a sore head to be civil, and off he went to cool himself in the salt water.

He and Jack stayed the best of friends, and Coo never did notice that the pots were empty. From that day on, Jack would find an excuse to nip down after every storm and free any poor souls that were caught. Some said that Jack Doherty saved more souls than any priest in Ireland, but I wouldn't know about that, now would I?

Oisín in Tír na nÓg

Fionn Mac Cumhail had only one son and his name was Oisín. Like his father before him, Oisín grew to be a great warrior, but it was for his songs and stories that he was famous in Ireland, for none sang more sweetly nor played the harp more gracefully.

The main reason, though, that Oisín will be remembered, is because it was he, alone of all mortal men, who went to Tír na nÓg, the Land of Eternal Youth, and returned to tell the tale.

One summer's day, Fionn and Oisín were out hunting on the shores of a great lake. Suddenly, a beautiful maiden appeared before them, riding a snow white horse. Her dress of silk was spangled with stars, her hair shimmered like gold, and on her head she wore the crown of a princess.

As she drew near, the maiden spoke. "So I've found you at last, Fionn Mac Cumhail," said she. "I've traversed the world to meet you."

"What is your name, young woman?" asked Fionn. "And where are you from?"

"I am Niamh of the Golden Hair," replied the princess, "and I have come from Tír na nÓg, where my father is king."

"Welcome to Erin, Princess Niamh," said Fionn. "But why have you come all this way to find me?"

"For the love of your son, Oisín," replied the maiden. "Much have I heard of his strength and his courage, and more have I heard of his stories and songs."

Niamh turned to Oisín. "Will you not return with me, my love? My land is fair above all others, and there we shall live, forever young and happy."

And Oisín, who had been silent all this time said, "I will go with you even to the ends of the earth, Niamh, for the moment I laid eyes on you I almost died with love."

Oisín kissed his father on the cheek and said goodbye, but Fionn wept. "I am sad that you are leaving, my son," he said, "for I fear we'll never meet again."

Oisín tried to comfort his father by promising to return, but Fionn would have none of it.

The young man then mounted the fairy horse behind Niamh, and they rode off to the sea. When they reached the shore, the horse neighed three times and leapt ahead. The waves opened before them and closed behind them and they rode so fast that they overtook the wind itself.

After a while, the sky darkened, the wind grew stronger, the waves rose high around them, thunder rolled and lightning flashed across the sky. But the white horse rode on through the storm until at last the sun was shining once more and Oisín saw that they were nearing the shores of a fair country.

Golden yellow was the sand, freshly green the grass, and tall

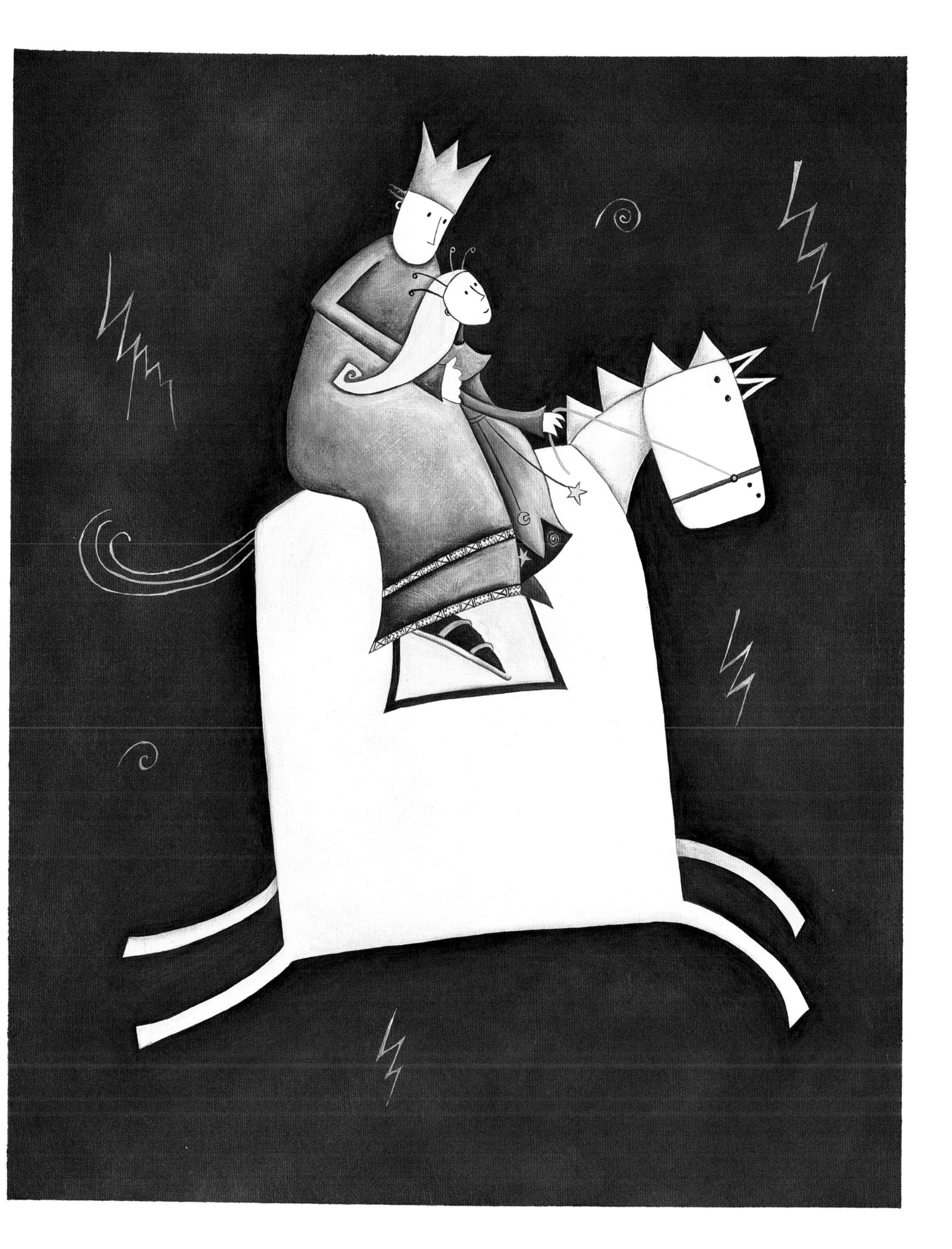

straight trees pointed up to the clear blue sky. There were hills and plains and flashing streams and in the distance, Oisín could make out a palace set with jewels, all glittering in the sunlight.

"Where are we?" asked Oisín. "For I've never seen a land as wonderful as this."

"This is Tír na nÓg," Niamh replied, "and that's the palace of the king, my father. I know you'll be happy here, Oisín."

As Niamh and Oisín climbed down from the fairy horse, a great crowd of people came to greet them. Joyfully, they were led to the palace, where the king and queen were waiting.

"A thousand welcomes to the Land of Youth, Oisín, son of Fionn," said the king. "The fame of your courage and your songs has already reached us, and I am pleased to have you here with us, where you shall live forever, young and happy."

Then Oisín was filled with gladness, and he and the fair princess were wed. There was a great feast, and although Oisín had seen many a feast in Erin, there had never been one like this.

For three hundred years, Oisín and Niamh lived happily in the

palace of the City of Youth, though to Oisín it felt no more than three, for a year seemed but a day in Tír na nÓg. They swam in warm lakes, raced their horses on the sand, and spent long balmy nights in each other's arms. If there was anything Oisín wished for, it appeared before him, and sweet music such as no mortal had ever heard wafted on the breeze.

But with everything so beautiful, and no one thing more lovely than another, Oisín felt no wish to sing or to play his harp. Sometimes he would long to go hunting, and often he would sigh when he thought of his father and the friends he had left behind in the land of Erin, but he didn't say anything to Niamh, for fear he would sound ungrateful.

Then one day he could stand it no more. "Hasn't your father any enemies I could fight?" he asked her. "Or wrongs I could put right? I'm a warrior, and I miss putting my sword to good use."

So Niamh told him of a beautiful princess in the Land of Virtue, which lay next to the Land of Youth. The princess had been captured by a fierce giant, Fovor of the Mighty Blows. He was holding her prisoner, in the hope that she would consent to marry him, but she had refused. The young princess was waiting for a knight to come and release her, but no one in Tír na nÓg or the Land of Virtue was brave enough to do so.

"I will fight the giant and free the beautiful princess!" cried Oisín. "Nothing would give me greater joy."

So the next morning, Oisín and Niamh rode out for the giant's castle. They rode all day through the mountains, and as they went, the path became steeper and the countryside less fair.

When they came to the castle, Oisín saw that it was a dark and evil looking place, with a large rusty horn hanging beside the gate. He rode up, blew the horn three times, and waited while the sound echoed through the valley. Slowly the gates creaked open, and Niamh and Oisín passed through them. An old and ugly serving man led them into the hall, where they found the beautiful princess, chained to the wall with seven chains.

"It's all right," said Niamh to the poor girl, when the serving man left them alone for a minute. "We've come to help you. Oisín here is going to fight the giant and free you from his power."

The princess wept for joy at this, for she had been held a prisoner for many months. "Be careful," she said, "for Fovor is cunning as well as strong."

"Don't worry," said Oisín, "giants are no match for the Fianna."

And with that, he went out into the courtyard, where Fovor, dressed ready for battle, was waiting for him.

The fight raged long and fierce. At first it looked as though

the giant would win, for he drove Oisín hard into a corner. But then Oisín thought of the poor princess chained to the wall. The anger rose within him, and with a yell he dived between Fovor's legs, spun around and clattered him a mighty blow that threw his opponent senseless to the ground.

The wounded giant was carried away, and one of the seven chains that held the maiden captive snapped and hung loosely by the wall.

The next day, Oisín and the giant fought again, and Oisín was again the victor. A second chain snapped and hung by the wall.

So it went on for seven days, and at the end of that time, the last chain broke and the princess was free.

"Thank you, thank you, thank you," she cried, throwing her arms around Oisín. "You are the bravest man in the Lands of Youth and Virtue and I shall be forever in your debt."

And with that the princess left to be with her own people, and Oisín and Niamh rode back to the palace of the City of Youth.

When he returned, Oisín was glad of heart, and he wished to celebrate his victory as in the old days in Erin. He opened his mouth to sing, but found no words. Somehow it felt wrong to sing of triumph in this land of beauty, where all was happiness and no man was better than another. Again, Oisín felt a great longing to visit Erin and see Fionn, his father, and the men of the Fianna once more.

So Oisín spoke to his wife, saying, "Niamh, my love, my heart is sore with desire to visit Erin. I pray you to let me return for a short time, for I promised my father that I would visit him one day, and I wish to sing to my people of the wonders of Tír na nÓg."

A chill ran through Niamh's heart when she heard these words, and she held Oisín tightly and tried to persuade him to change his mind. But at length she saw that her husband would always be unhappy if she did not let him go, so she agreed.

The next morning, Niamh saddled the white horse with her own hands and brought it to him. "Go to Erin if you must," she said, with tears in her eyes. "My horse will carry you safely over the sea and back again, but do not for a moment get down from the saddle. If you set foot on Irish soil, even for an instant, you will never return to the Land of Youth!"

Oisín kissed his wife and said goodbye, vowing that he'd stay on the horse. Then he rode away over the sea, and after many days he arrived.

But his heart sank when he reached Erin, for it didn't look anything like the country he had left. The rivers were deeper, the hills were lower, there were strange little cottages dotted all around, with small weak men working in the fields. And when he came to the hill of Tara, where Fionn's castle had once stood, all had

changed. The hill rose up as before, but the castle was in ruins, already half-buried by weeds and briars. Oisín was filled with sadness, for he could not understand what had happened to his land and his people.

A little farther on, he came to some of the little men, struggling with all their might to lift a huge flagstone. They had succeeded in half raising it, but the weight of the slab was so great that the men underneath were being crushed.

"Help! Help!" they cried, when they saw the mighty Oisín riding near.

Oisín couldn't believe that so many men were powerless to move a single stone. "You're not the Fianna, for sure!" said he, laughing. He leaned over in his saddle and, taking the full weight of the flagstone in his hands, he raised it and flung it away, freeing the men beneath.

But the next moment the men's cries of relief turned to shouts of fear. For Oisín's effort had been so great that the golden belt around his horse's stomach had snapped, pulling him out of the saddle. As he hit the ground, Niamh's warning screamed in his ears, but it was too late.

The great white horse vanished as mist before the midday sun, and the men watched in horror as the tall young warrior's powerful body withered and shrank, and his skin sagged into wrinkles and folds. Instead of a handsome knight they saw only a blind old man, bent with the weight of many hundreds of years, lying helpless at their feet.

Running to help him, they asked him who and what he was. But when he told them that he was Oisín, son of Fionn, they laughed and said, "You must be mad, old man. Fionn Mac Cumhail is dead and gone these three hundred years, and all his company with him. A holy man called Patrick has come to Ireland and we are all Christians now."

So they took him to Saint Patrick, who listened to Oisín and treated him kindly, for he could see that the old man had not long to live in this world.

Oisín told Patrick the tales of Fionn and the Fianna for the very last time, and the saint listened with wonder. He asked his monks to write them down, so they might not be forgotten. They put them into a beautiful book, with drawings on every page, and the final story was the tale of Oisín in Tír na nÓg.

So put a sod on the fire, give an apple to the child, and pour a drink for the storyteller.

Sources

The Irish storytelling tradition is one of the richest in the world. Because the Romans did not invade Ireland, the spoken language has remained relatively unchanged, and this is one of the reasons why so many early Irish legends have survived. Later, the early Christian church in Ireland respected the traditions of the local people, creating a situation that was without parallel in the countries of Europe.

Stories and poems were passed down through the generations by word of mouth. Many more would have disappeared but for the work of Irish monks in the seventh and eighth centuries. They recorded as many of the old tales as they could find, mostly myths and legends of the early Celtic warriors. Although many of these writings were lost or destroyed over the next few centuries through wars or raids by the Vikings, enough survived for further copies to be made in the eleventh and twelfth centuries, and it is from these that the oldest of the stories I have included in this anthology are taken.

Much later, in the nineteenth century, there was a great reawakening of interest in folklore, and collectors toured around rural Ireland gathering stories and songs, mostly in the Irish language. Included in this collection are my retellings of tales gathered at that time by Thomas Crofton Croker, Patrick Kennedy and Jeremiah Curtin, as well as one collected more recently by Sean O'Sullivan.

The Children of Lir

The Children of Lir, one of the "three sorrows of storytelling," is probably the best-loved Irish folk tale. Edna O'Brien comments in her book *Mother Ireland* (Weidenfeld and Nicholson, London 1976) that "learning the jargon about the proud and melodious swans" is part and parcel of growing up in Ireland. There is a beautiful bronze sculpture of the children in the Garden of Remembrance in Dublin, made by Oisín Kelly. The children are falling, as if from a blow, while four swans are rising up from them, representing Ireland's struggle for independence.

Lir was one of the five great lords of the Tuatha Dé Danaan, and the story was first set down by monks in the fifteenth century, although it is believed to date back to the pre-Celtic oral tradition. The original version is unlikely, therefore, to have included references to Saint Patrick and the coming of Christianity to Ireland.

The Children of Lir comes from the first main cycle of Irish literature, the Mythological Cycle. Most of the stories in this cycle refer to the battle for supremacy between the Tuatha Dé Danaan, the people of the goddess Danu, and the Fomorians, a race of demons who lived on offshore islands. The Tuatha Dé Danaan are said to have inhabited Ireland in pre-Christian times, until they were defeated by the Milesians, the ancestors of the present inhabitants. Despite their great power in both music and magic, the Tuatha Dé Danaan were driven underground, where they became the fairies.

Fair, Brown and Trembling

The great American collector, Jeremiah Curtin, heard this story in 1887, and included it in his *Myths and Folklore of Ireland* (Little, Brown, Boston 1890). Curtin, the son of Irish immigrants, came from Wisconsin. He was an expert on American Indian mythology and could read seventy languages. Curtin visited the West of Ireland in 1887 and 1892 to record wonder tales, stories of ghosts and fairies and tales of the Fianna. He was probably the best of the early collectors, for he gathered stories in the Irish language and translated them accurately, without adding a literary or mock-Irish voice. *Fair, Brown and Trembling* is clearly a version of the Cinderella story, common throughout the world.

The Twelve Wild Geese

The Twelve Wild Geese was included in *The Fireside Stories of Ireland*, by Patrick Kennedy (McGlashan and Gill, Dublin 1870). Kennedy loved the old folk tales of Ireland, but feared that through famine, emigration, the growth of literacy and the decline of the Irish language, the oral tradition might be lost. When he became a Dublin bookseller, therefore, he put together several excellent collections of the stories he remembered from his childhood in the hills of County Wexford. *The Twelve Wild Geese* is an example of an international wonder tale, occurring in many traditions — the Grimm brothers recorded a version known as *The Six Swans*.

Lusmore and the Fairies

Also known as *The Legend of Knockgrafton*, this story was collected by Thomas Crofton Croker and printed in volume one of his *Fairy Legends and Traditions of the South of Ireland* (John Murray, London 1825–28). This was the first collection of folk tales in the British Isles taken directly from the oral tradition. The book was a great success, and within a year the Grimm brothers had translated it into German, under the title *Irische Elfenmärchen*. There are many stories of fairies gathering at raths or mounds, and Croker was told this tale within view of the mound of Knockgrafton in August 1816. Fairies must be dealt with respectfully, and this story is a warning of the dangers of not doing so. In his book, Crofton Croker gives a tune for their song, which he says was "commonly sung by every skilful narrator of the tale." The word "lusmore" literally means the great herb, and is the Irish for foxglove, sometimes called fairy cap by country people on account of the shape of its petals. There are many European versions of this story, including Italian, Breton and Spanish, and it appears in Seki's *Folktales of Japan* (Routledge and Kegan Paul, Chicago and London 1963).

Son of an Otter, Son of a Wolf

I have adapted this from *The King Who Could Not Sleep* in Sean O'Sullivan's wonderful book, *Folktales of Ireland* (University of Chicago Press, Chicago 1966). O'Sullivan, chief archivist of the Irish Folklore Commission from its establishment in 1935 until 1973, played a crucial role in recording the oral tradition. This one was collected in Irish from Jimmy Cheallaigh in the parish of Glenfin, County Donegal in 1934. In his book *The Types of the Irish Folktale* (Seán Ó Súilleabhain and Reider Th. Christiansen, Soumalainen Tiedeakatemia, Helsinki 1967), O'Sullivan lists twenty-five versions of the tale. The Irish Folklore Commission is now known as the Department of Irish Folklore, and is housed at University College, Dublin. The richness of its archives, more than one-and-a-half-million pages, makes it the envy of the world.

The Soul Cages

The Soul Cages was published by Thomas Crofton Croker in his *Fairy Legends and Traditions of the South of Ireland*. Crofton Croker, however, had borrowed the story from Thomas Keightley, another collector, without giving him credit for it. When Keightley protested in public, Crofton Croker confined himself in later editions to tales he'd personally collected. In his book *The Fairy Mythology* (H.G.Bohn, London 1828), Keightley confessed that the story had not been collected in the field, in fact, but was partly based on a German tale found by the Brothers Grimm, and partly his own invention. He also noted, confusingly, that the tale was well known on the coast of Cork and Wicklow at the time of publication. The German tale has been translated by Donald Ward as *The Merman and the Farmer*, and is included in the *German Legends of the Brothers Grimm* (Institute for the Study of Human Issues, Philadelphia 1981).

Oisín in Tír na nÓg

The final story in my book tells of Oisín and the time he spent in Tír na nÓg, the Land of Youth. It comes at the very end of the Fenian Cycle, the great cycle of stories about the legendary Fionn Mac Cumhail and his band of followers, the Fianna. Although mythical heroes such as Fionn are unlikely to have actually existed, they are probably based on real warrior champions, and the stories give us a unique insight into the general structure of Irish society at the time. Oisín's eventual friendship with Saint Patrick is a powerful symbol of the reconciliation of paganism and Christianity, a major factor in the survival to this day of these wonderful stories.